My
Off-Limits
Protector Next
Door

EVA STONE

Contents

I Will Marry You

"What's your name?" the ten-year-old girl in my arms asks, her voice barely above a whisper against the crackling backdrop of the burning house.

"Alex Jones," I reply, trying to mask my concern calmly as I navigate the smoky chaos.

"I'm Julia," she says, her tiny fingers clutching my jacket. "I will marry you when I grow up, Mr. Jones." Her innocent and sincere words momentarily distract me from the roaring inferno.

As the paramedics take her from my arms, her declaration lingers in my mind. It's the first time anyone has said something like that to me. At twenty, I'm more familiar with the heat of fires than the warmth of such words.

However, it's just a kid's way of saying thanks.

In the weeks following the fire, Julia regularly visits the station. She always comes bearing gifts—small tokens of gratitude. The latest is a Christmas candy jar brimming with festive treats, which she proudly shares with my crew.

"Merry Christmas, everyone!" She beams, excitement filling the station more than the bright lights and decorations adorning the walls.

The guys, a tough bunch, softened by her presence, gather around to partake in the sweets. I lean against my fire truck, watching the scene unfold with a smile I can't entirely suppress.

"And this," Julia announces, turning towards me with a smaller, carefully wrapped package, "is for you, Alex."

She hands me a homemade cupcake, the icing a bit uneven but made with undeniable care. "I made it myself," she adds, her eyes seeking approval.

"Thank you, Julia," I say, genuinely touched. "It looks great."

My crew doesn't miss a beat. "Looks like Alex has got himself a little sweetheart!" they tease. Laughter echoes around the station, but I shake my head, chuckling.

"She's just a little friend, guys," I protest, but it's a feeble attempt.

Julia, unfazed by the teasing, stands with quiet confidence. "I wanted to thank Alex for saving me," she states, and I'm struck by her resilience, her spirit.

The station, usually resonant with the sound of alarms and the rumble of engines, is filled with a different energy during her visits. Her curiosity about our work and her endless questions about firefighting bring a lightness to our routine.

I reflect as the afternoon fades and Julia's mom arrives to pick her up. I've always seen myself as just an ordinary guy, easily overlooked. But through Julia's eyes, I'm reminded that sometimes, being ordinary can still mean being someone's hero.

I watch their car disappear down the street, the cupcake in my hand a simple, sweet reminder of the unexpected bonds that life can bring.

Three years have passed since I first met Julia in the burning fire.

Today marks my twenty-third birthday, which starts just like any other day at the fire station—filled with the usual drills and the background hum of radios. But there's an undercurrent of excitement among the crew; I can tell they've been planning something.

The surprise comes at midmorning. Julia bursts through the doors, her face bright with a smile that could light up the gloomiest day. She carries a clumsily wrapped gift, her steps hurried, eager.

"Happy Birthday, Alex!" she exclaims, presenting the gift with a flourish. I grin at her enthusiasm.

"Thanks, Julia. You don't have to," I add, but I'm genuinely pleased.

She's grown so much since I carried her out of the fire that night. She's almost a teenager now.

But today, there's another figure trailing behind her, hesitantly pushing open the station door. Luby, my girlfriend of six months, steps in, her eyes scanning the room before landing on me.

"Hey, Birthday Boy," Luby says, a hint of a smile on her lips. She's holding a store-bought cake. I know her attempt at a gesture doesn't come quickly to her.

Luby works in sales at Dillard's. She's lovely and usually stands out in a crowd, sparkling with charisma. But today, around my buddies, she seems shy, a side of her I rarely see.

The room's warmth dissipates as Julia's bright smile falters, her gaze flickering between me and Luby. There's a trace of something in her eyes—confusion, maybe, or a tinge of disappointment that didn't belong on a young girl's face.

"Who's she?" Julia's question cuts through the muffled sounds of the station, her voice climbing a notch, unsteady.

"This is Luby, my girlfriend," I introduce, aiming for a casual tone to ease the sudden tension.

Luby extends a polite smile, a practiced curve of her lips that doesn't quite reach her eyes.

Julia's response is a simple, elongated, "Oh," laden with unspoken words, the kind that hover and thicken the air. I catch a flicker of something—a shadow, a thought, a feeling—crossing her face before she masks it with a semblance of neutrality.

The birthday celebration continues, but we're all actors in a poorly rehearsed play. Julia's vibrant energy, usually so infectious, is subdued. She picks at her cupcake, glances towards Luby, and is loaded with a complexity that seems beyond her years.

At one point, I find myself standing beside her, trying to bridge the widening gap with small talk. "You know, Julia, having more people in our lives just means there's more love to go around," I say, hoping to lighten her mood.

She looks up at me, her eyes searching mine for an answer to a question she hasn't asked. "Does it? Sometimes it seems like it just divides it up, makes it... less," she says, her words striking a chord deep inside me.

When it's time for her to leave, I say, "See you, Julia."

Julia's eyes carefully avoid mine as if she fears what they might reveal. "I don't want to say 'see you,' Alex."

I watch her go. A part of me wants to call her back, but I think she is too young to understand my explanation. She's just a little girl.

Since then, Julia has never shown up at the fire station.

Christmas rolls around, and instead of Julia's usual visit, I find a card in the mail, signed simply, "From Julia." It's a small gesture, but it speaks volumes of the distance growing between us.

Life, as it does, keeps moving. My relationship with Luby deepens. We become a couple, a step that feels both exciting and daunting.

Luby is different from anyone I've ever known—independent, strong-willed, with a social circle that spans the entire city.

Our home has become a hub of activity, with friends and acquaintances coming and going. Luby is always at the center, vibrant and lively.

I adapt to this new life, the quiet firefighter in a world of loud personalities.

Yet, in quiet moments, when the noise fades, and I'm alone with my thoughts, I miss my quiet world.

As the years pass, those Christmas cards become the only constants from Julia. Eventually, she faded from my busy life.

***

Now, at thirty, my life looks different.

I've been married to Luby for six years, and we have two kids: Kim is two years old, and Jim is about five. They are the center of my world. But honestly, it's not the happy picture everyone sees from the outside.

Luby, with her vibrant personality and never-ending social energy, is the star of our neighborhood. She's the one who knows everyone's business, from who's expecting a baby to the latest gossip about someone's rocky marriage.

At dinner, she's always animated, sharing stories and news. At the same time, I find myself just listening, often feeling like a spectator in my own life.

"Did you hear about the Thompsons? They're finally getting a pool," she'd say, her eyes sparkling with excitement. I'd just nod, my mind drifting away from the gossip. Instead, I'm thinking about Kim needing a new shoe or Jim's latest painting, still stuck on the fridge, full of vibrant colors and childlike imagination.

"Alex, are you even listening?" Luby's voice snaps me back to the present.

"Sorry, just tired from work," I mumble, forcing a smile. But the truth is, it's more than just physical exhaustion. It's this growing sense of disconnection from Luby, from the life we've built together.

"I see." Luby hands me a bowl of soup. "Hey, Alex, are you attending the Hendersons' party next Saturday?" Luby's voice is tinged with excitement, as she flips through a magazine filled with party themes. Her eyes don't leave the glossy pages, but I know she's expecting a positive response.

I pause, then say, "I... might have a shift, Luby," my voice trailing off, unsure.

The thought of another social event, another night of forced smiles and small talk, weighs heavily on me.

She looks up, her expression shifting to mild frustration, a crease forming between her brows. "Alex. You are just a captain, but you are busier than the mayor. You know when you're here, you're not 'here'?" Her words, though spoken softly, hit hard. They're a reminder of the gap that's been growing between us.

"I know, I'm sorry. But I'm not a party fan," I reply, a familiar sense of guilt settling in my chest.

In less than ten minutes since I came to the dining table, I have already apologized more than ten times.

I watch her reaction closely.

Luby sighs, a slight frown creasing her forehead as she returns to the magazine. In that brief exchange, a moment of potential connection flickers and then fades, slipping away as quickly as it appeared. The gap between us widens a little more.

Later, as I sit on the couch, the TV sounds are just dull background noise, and I reflect on my days. With its relentless demands and unexpected emergencies, the job used to feel fulfilling. Coming home was the relief, the comfort.

But now, home feels like stepping into a foreign land where I'm constantly trying to find my footing.

Luby is there, but we live parallel lives under the same roof. Her world revolves around social events and maintaining appearances. At the same time, mine is about life-and-death decisions and the chaos of emergencies.

I glance over at Luby, who's now animatedly talking on the phone, likely planning another event. I stand up, needing to escape to find some cool night air.

Before I walk out, I hear a little voice.

"Can you put us to bed tonight, Daddy?" Kim's small voice is full of hope as she tugs at my sleeve one evening.

"Of course, sweetheart," I reply, grateful for the chance to escape the noise and be with my kids.

But as I sit there, reading bedtime stories in their dimly lit room, I can't shake off the feeling of being out of place everywhere else. I love my family and want to be a good husband and father. But with each passing day, I feel like I'm losing a part of myself, a part that Luby and I used to share.

***

I'm jolted awake by Luby's laughter, ringing loud and clear through the house. She's on the phone, her voice bubbling with excitement. I glance at the clock—it's earlier than I'd hoped to be up on my day off. Rubbing my eyes, I try to cling to the remnants of sleep, but it's futile.

She sees me stirring and immediately switches gears. "Alex, let's go shopping today." Her tone is cheerful, leaving no room for argument.

I groan inwardly. Shopping with Luby is an all-day affair, especially when she's hunting for something specific—like the perfect dress for the Hendersons' party. And I know it means the kids and I will spend hours trailing after her in the store.

By midday, we're deep in the throes of her shopping spree. The kids are restless and hungry; I'm tired and overwhelmed by the endless parade of dresses Luby keeps trying on. She flits from one mirror to another, her energy undiminished.

"What do you think of this one, Alex?" she asks, twirling in front of the mirrors.

I offer a halfhearted thumbs-up, my attention divided between her and keeping an eye on Kim and Jim, who are getting more fidgety by the minute.

"This is your payback for not coming to the party," Luby jokes, but her voice has an edge that makes me wince.

I want to find Kim a new pair of shoes—she's been needing them for weeks—but Luby's preoccupied with dress after dress. I glance at Kim, her small face looking up at me with boredom and hope.

"Soon, sweetheart," I whisper to her, but I'm unsure when.

By the end of the day, we've spent nearly $450. The party dress costs $360, and the rest goes to dining out. But seeing Luby's glowing face, her happiness is evident in every smile and laugh.

It's clear that the expense is justified to her, even though she already has more than enough clothes hanging in the closet. Each new addition brings her joy, contrasting my more practical view of necessities. As I watch her admire her latest purchase, I can't help but tally the cost, both monetary and in terms of the time and energy spent, wondering if it's all worth it.

Sitting next to Luby at the restaurant, I feel disconnected, wondering how our perspectives on something as simple as clothing can vastly differ.

Soon, my birthday arrives. Luby confronts me before I head off to work, her voice strained with frustration. "I've invited everyone, Alex. Can't you skip just this once?" she pleads.

I nod first and then shake my head, a heavy feeling settling in my chest. "I wish I could, but you know I can't guarantee it," I reply, the weight of my duty as a firefighter making it impossible to acquiesce.

As the sun sets, casting long shadows over the city, my phone buzzes insistently in my pocket. I'm just minutes away from home to attend my birthday party, but the moment I see the caller ID—it's the fire chief—I know that any plans I have are about to change.

"Jones," I answer, my voice automatically shifting to a tone of readiness.

"Captain, there's a fire, residential, on Fifth Street. It's near a factory. We need all hands," comes my chief's brisk, urgent reply.

My heart sinks, but duty overrides personal disappointment. "On my way," I respond, already turning the car around.

As I approach the scene, the sky is painted with ominous plumes of smoke. The fire has engulfed a two-story house, flames licking hungrily at the walls, threatening to spread to neighboring homes. The street is chaotic, filled with the noise of sirens and the shouts of my fellow firefighters.

As captain, I quickly put on my turnout gear and take charge of my teams.

"Listen up," I say, my voice steady and clear, "we need to sweep the building and ensure everyone's out. Reports suggest someone might be trapped on the second floor!"

My team nods in unison, their faces set with determination. We've trained for this, and we move as a cohesive unit under my leadership. The heat from the burning building is almost a physical barrier, but we push through it, our focus unwavering.

As we enter the building, the smoke is like a thick fog, reducing visibility to nearly zero. I lead the way upstairs, the heat intensifying with each step. The structure groans ominously under our boots, a stark reminder of the risks inherent in every step.

"Fire department, call out if you can hear me!" I yell, my voice echoing through the smoky haze.

Then, a faint sound—a cough. My trained ears pick it up immediately. I signal my team and head towards the source, a small room clouded with smoke. There, under a window, is a young woman and a little girl, their eyes wide with fear.

I reach them quickly, my presence offering her some comfort. "I've got you," I assure them, my voice calm and confident even through the mask. Gently, I lift the girl into my arms, her weight light but her grip tight, a silent testament to her fear.

I look at the young lady, urgency apparent in my eyes. "Follow me, quickly," I instruct, guiding her towards the stairs. As we start descending, two other firefighters, part of my team, join us. They move in swiftly, one leading the way and the other following behind us, ensuring we have support on both sides as we navigate through the smoke and potential hazards. Together, we work as a unit, focused on getting them to safety as efficiently as possible.

"Team, we're coming out. Prepare for extraction," I communicate through my radio, leading the way back through the treacherous, smoky passageways with the victim in my arms.

Every second is crucial; the building could collapse at any moment. But it's more than just a job for me; it's a commitment, a vow to protect and save lives, no matter the danger. As we emerge into the night, the cool air hitting us like a wave, I know that this is what being a captain is all about—leading from the front, saving lives, and bringing my team back safely.

Back outside, the cool night air is a stark contrast to the inferno inside. Paramedics take the woman and the girl. Now, they are safe.

My phone buzzes again with a message from Luby. I know it will be filled with disappointment and frustration.

When I return home, exhausted and longing for rest, the aftermath of the missed party hits me in full force. The house is quiet; Kim and Jim are already in their beds. But Luby's anger is loud and clear. Her disappointment manifests in a heated argument, louder and more intense than any we've had before.

"You missed your own birthday party, Alex!" Luby's voice is sharp, a cutting edge that slices through my exhaustion. "Do you know how embarrassing it was to explain to everyone why you weren't there?"

I lean against the wall, feeling the tension in my shoulders tighten. "There was a fire, Luby. Someone's life was in danger. I couldn't just leave—" I begin, my voice weary yet firm.

"But there's always a fire, isn't there? Always some emergency!" Her hands are on her hips, her stance rigid with frustration. "What about the emergency here, at home? What about us?"

Luby steps closer, her voice tinged with frustration and disappointment. "Do you know how many hours I spent cooking in the kitchen for your birthday meal?"

I run a hand through my hair, struggling to find words to bridge the chasm between our worlds. "I'm a firefighter, Luby. This is what I signed up for. Saving lives—it's not just a job, it's a calling."

"A calling?" Luby scoffs, her voice rising. "What about your calling as a husband, as a father? Do those mean anything to you?"

The accusation stings more than the heat of any fire I've faced. "Of course they do," I shoot back, my frustration bubbling up. "But I can't control when emergencies happen. I wish I could be in two places simultaneously, but I can't!"

Luby's expression hardens, her eyes glinting with unshed tears of anger and hurt. "Sometimes I wonder if you even want to be with us."

That hits a nerve, and I'm at a loss for words for a moment. The gap in understanding between us feels more comprehensive than ever. I'm torn between my duty and my love for my family, and it's a balance I'm constantly struggling to maintain.

"I always want to be here," I say quietly, the fight draining out of me. "But I also can't turn my back on people who need me—"

I stop midsentence as I notice Jim and Kim standing in the hallway. Their faces are etched with fear and confusion, clearly scared by the intensity of our exchange. This moment brings a stark realization of how our conflicts resonate beyond just the two of us, touching the innocent lives we are responsible for.

The room falls into a heavy silence, our words hanging like smoke. At that moment, it's clear that the fire I fight at work isn't the only blaze I'm struggling to contain. The fire at home, burning through my marriage, is proving to be just as challenging, if not more so. And right now, I'm not sure how to extinguish it.

In the end, I lay on the couch, alone in the dim light of the living room. Though sharing the same roof, Luby and I are worlds apart, sleeping with different dreams and growing frustrations.

Lying there, I can't shake off the guilt that clings to me, heavier with each passing day. I love my family, but the rift between Luby and me seems to widen with every missed party and every unshared moment. I'm caught in a constant battle between my duties as a firefighter and a husband, feeling like I'm failing at both.

As the night stretches on, I'm left with my thoughts, the house's silence amplifying the sense of disconnection that's become my constant companion. The joy of family life I once longed for now feels like a distant dream, slipping further away with each passing day.

The air in our home carries a weight, thick with unspoken words and the echoes of recent arguments. It feels as if the walls themselves have absorbed the tension, the sadness.

We're on the path to divorce.

***

This evening, we sit across from each other at the kitchen table, feeling like we're facing strangers.

"Alex, I need more than this," Luby says, breaking the silence, her voice firm yet tinged with unmistakable weariness. "I've spent six years waiting for you to change—they were the best years of my life. I can't do it anymore."

I look at her, the woman I once thought I'd spend my entire life with, now a stranger in her home. "Luby, isn't there a way we can make this work?" My voice is a plea, a last grasp at a slipping thread.

She looks down, then up again, her eyes sad. "No, Alex. We are done," Luby says, her voice devoid of the warmth it once held. "I need to find out who I am, find a better man, and live a better life."

Her words are sharp, cutting through any remaining hope of reconciliation. They echo in the room, a stark testament to the end of what we once had.

"What about Kim and Jim?" I worry about our kids. They are so young.

"I love them, I really do. But I'm just so lost, Alex. I need space to make my life better. The kids will be okay with you." Luby's voice is firm, but her eyes tell a different story. There's pain there.

"They're both so young," I say, thinking about how much they need their mother.

"Being young is better. Kids won't remember much or hurt as much as I do." Luby lifts her chin, trying to sound confident.

Her words are like a punch in the gut. She's so distant, even talking about our own kids. That's when I know for sure—I need to be the one who's there for Kim and Jim. They deserve a fully present parent who cares about their every little need.

Over the next few days, Luby packs up her things. The kids are confused, not really understanding what's happening. I try to explain, but it's hard. They just look at me, not really getting it.

So now, I'm a single dad, navigating a world that feels familiar and alien. Each morning is a battle, a juggling act of preparing breakfast, packing lunchboxes, and double-checking that Kim and Jim have everything they need for preschool and kindergarten.

The house, once filled with Luby's laughter and endless chatter, now echoes with the sounds of children's shows and the occasional bickering of siblings. The chair where Luby used to sit at dinner is now just an empty space. Her side of the bed is cold and untouched.

I try to fill these gaps with extra love for Kim and Jim—more hugs, longer bedtime stories, and forced smiles. But their little eyes often wander to that empty chair, filled with questions they can't put into words.

One night, I walk down the hallway to check on Kim and Jim. I gently push Kim's bedroom door open and see her curled up on her little bed. In the soft glow of her nightlight, I notice her small arms clutching something tightly to her chest. I move closer, treading softly to avoid waking her, and realize that she's holding on to one of Luby's old sleeping shirts.

The sight is both tender and heart-wrenching.

I stand there for a moment, watching her. These quiet, unguarded moments reveal the depth of the kids' feelings and the silent struggle they face in understanding the changes in our family. I feel a mix of emotions—sadness for their loss, anger at Luby for leaving this void, and a fierce determination to be all that my children need.

Quietly, I walk over and gently adjust the blanket around Kim, careful not to disturb her. Leaning down, I whisper a soft "I love you," hoping my presence can offer comfort, even as she sleeps.

I step back and take another look at Kim. She's still holding her mom's shirt. In the quiet light of her room, I promise myself again, not just to be there for her and Jim but to help them feel better, to help them understand and get through this tough time. It's a big job, but I'm ready to do it. They mean everything to me, and I'll do whatever I can to make them feel okay again.

The days leading up to Luby's visits are the toughest. Kim and Jim mark off the days on the calendar, their excitement growing.

"Daddy, only two more days until Mommy comes!" Kim exclaims one morning, her eyes bright with joy.

"Yeah, I can't wait to show her my new drawing," Jim adds, his voice filled with a rare enthusiasm.

I smile at their happiness, though some of me dreads Luby's commitment unpredictability. Then, my phone buzzes. It's a text from Luby: I am on vacation with my boyfriend, so I won't make it for the visit.

I look up at Kim and Jim, their expectant faces making this even more complex. "Kids, I just got a message from Mommy," I start, my voice gentle.

"She's not coming, is she?" Kim asks.

"No, honey, not this time. Mom's... away," I say, trying to keep my voice steady.

Jim's face falls instantly, his disappointment a tangible thing. "But she promised," he murmurs.

Kim turns away, tears in her eyes.

I kneel to their level, feeling a surge of protectiveness. "I know, and I'm sorry. But how about we do something special instead? Just the three of us?" I suggest trying to salvage their spirits.

"Can we make pancakes for dinner?" Kim asks a slight quiver in her voice.

"And watch a movie?" Jim adds, still not looking up.

"Absolutely," I reply, wrapping them both in a hug. "We'll make it a fun night, I promise."

I have a happy day with Kim and Jim. As I tuck them in at bedtime, their little arms cling to me a bit tighter. "We love you, Daddy," they murmur, and my heart aches with love and pain.

I stare at the ceiling in bed, feeling glad the kids ended their day happily. Tomorrow will be another challenging day.

The following day is Sunday. Amidst the usual morning chaos, there's a knock at the door. I open it to find a young girl in her early twenties holding a pie. She has a friendly, familiar smile, but I can't place her.

"Hi, I'm Jane Willow, your new neighbor," she extends a pie towards me. "I thought I'd introduce myself."

I take the pie from her, noticing it's freshly baked and still warm in my hands, a bit surprised by this unexpected kindness. "Thanks, that's really kind of you. I'm Alex," I reply, stepping aside to let her in.

As she enters, her eyes briefly scan the living room—toys scattered, breakfast dishes on the table, a clear sign of our rushed life.

"You've got your hands full here," she remarks with a sympathetic smile.

"Yeah, it's been a bit hectic since... well, since I started doing this solo," I admit, feeling self-conscious about the mess.

Jane nods understandingly. "I work at Jim's elementary school. I see you dropping him off sometimes."

As I pour milk for Kim, I turn to Jane with curiosity. "What do you teach?" I ask.

Jim, overhearing our conversation, pipes up with a smile. "Ms. Willow is our art teacher," he says proudly.

Jane hesitates momentarily, then offers, "If it helps, I could take Jim to school. I'm heading that way anyway. It might make your mornings a little easier?"

I'm taken aback by her kindness. "That would be… actually, that would be a huge help. Thank you."

We chat a little more—Jane is easy to talk to, and something about her is reassuringly familiar. As she leaves, I feel a weight lifted off my shoulders.

A few weeks pass, and Jane's help with Jim has become a routine that I'm incredibly grateful for.

But the unpredictability of my job as a fire-fighter still looms large. One afternoon, I get an emergency call just as I'm supposed to pick up Kim from kindergarten. I rush to the scene, the stress of being late to pick up Kim gnawing at me.

By the time I'm done and rush to the YMCA to pick up Jim, I'm met with disapproving looks and a penalty for late pickup.

The next day, Jane notices my distress. "Rough day?" she asks gently.

I nod, explaining the situation. Jane listens. Her expression is thoughtful. "How about I pick up Jim and Kim whenever you need me? I can bring them home and care for them until you arrive. It's no trouble."

I'm overwhelmed by her offer. "I... I don't know what to say. That would be amazing."

I stand at the front door as Jane leaves, re-flecting on her kindness. It brings a warmth to my heart, a feeling that's been rare in these challenging times.

As time passes, Jane becomes more than just the lady next door who helps out. She's kind and easygoing with the kids—it's like she becomes a part of our everyday life. Gradually, I look forward to seeing her, to hearing her knock on the door. Her simple and warm smile makes everything feel a bit lighter for me.

One evening, duty calls me away unexpectedly, and I can't pick up Kim and Jim. Without a second thought, I dial Jane's number. "Jane, I'm sorry to ask, but could you—?"

"Don't worry, Alex. I'll pick them up," she answers without hesitation, her voice a soothing balm to my frayed nerves.

When I return home that night, the house is tidy and calm, unlike the usual mess. Jane's sitting by Kim and Jim's beds, reading them a story. Her voice is soft and sweet, filling the room with quiet peace. It's like looking at a cozy picture, everything calm and gentle.

In the kitchen, there's dinner ready on the table. It's nothing fancy, but Jane put her heart into making it.

Jane looks up as I enter, and in the soft lamp-light, her face holds a serene beauty that catches me off guard. She dresses simply, contrasting Luby's preference for makeup and high fashion. Her simplicity is elegant, a genuine quality that resonates deeply with me.

"Thanks, Jane. I don't know what I'd do without your help," I say with sincere gratitude.

"It's nothing, really. I enjoy it," Jane replies with a smile that reaches her eyes.

After the kids sleep, we sit at the dining table, discussing Jim's latest painting. Jane's eyes light up as she discusses his talent.

"Jim has a real gift," she says earnestly. "His use of color, his expression—it's remarkable for his age. He has a great imagination."

I watch her enthusiasm for Jim's hobby and her belief in him. My feelings for Jane begin to shift in these small, genuine moments. What starts as gratitude slowly blossoms into something more profound that surprises and scares me. I wasn't searching for love, yet it has found me in the most unexpected ways.

As Jane prepares to leave, I am reluctant to see her go.

There's a connection between us, subtle yet undeniable. It's a far cry from my tumultuous and passionate relationship with Luby. With Jane, it's like a quiet melody, soothing and reasoning.

That night, lying in bed, I couldn't stop thinking about Jane—how kind she is, how simply and beautifully she carries herself, and the quiet comfort she's brought into our lives. She's so different from Luby, with all the ups and downs we had. Being around Jane is soothing; she's gently healing all the hurt without even meaning to.

I start realizing that what I feel for her has changed, and grown into something bigger than I ever thought it would. It's scary but also exciting. After all the tough times, love has returned to me.

But this time, it's different with Jane. It's quiet, not showy, but deep and genuine.

My feelings for Jane deepen as time passes, but I hold back, wary of scaring her away. She's young, full of life and beauty, and in my eyes, she deserves someone far better than me. So, I tread carefully, keeping my growing affection under wraps.

Jane, perceptive as always, seems to sense the shift in my emotions. But she remains the same—a steadfast, caring friend, never over-stepping boundaries.

It's a delicate dance we're in, both aware of an undercurrent of something more, yet neither of us dare take the first step.

Then, one quiet evening, after the kids have drifted off to sleep, Jane turns to me with a seriousness I've not seen before. She hands me a folder with a mysterious smile.

Curious, I open it to find an old newspaper clip-ping—a picture of a firefighter holding a little girl. It's me, a decade ago, and Julia is the girl I saved from a fire.

Why does Jane show me this old newspaper?

"Alex, I need to tell you something," Jane starts, her voice barely above a whisper. "My first name is Julia. Jane is my middle name. I'm that girl you saved."

The revelation hits me like a wave. Julia—the little girl who promised to marry me, who visited the station, who drifted away... and now here she is, in front of me, as Jane.

She continues, her eyes locked on mine. "I've always seen you as my hero, the man who saved my life. I've admired you, cared for you, for as long as I can remember."

I sit there, stunned, trying to process the enormity of what she's saying. "You... you've been here all this time? Watching over me? Over us?"

Jane nods, her expression a mix of vulnerability and hope. "Alex, I need to ensure that I can bring happiness to you. And I needed to know if your kids could accept me."

The room feels like it's spinning, my mind racing to piece together all the moments and interactions with Jane—no, Julia.

The care, the connection, the unexplained familiarity—it all makes sense now.

I look at her, really look at her, seeing not just the neighbor, not just the woman who's become a friend, but Julia, the girl who grew up holding on to a memory, a promise.

"Julia," I call her name.

Her name feels both new and familiar on my lips. "I... I don't know what to say. You've been right here, and I...."

Words fail me, but the emotions don't. I reach out, pulling Julia into a hug, feeling the pieces of a puzzle I didn't even know were missing falling into place.

We hold each other, and in that embrace, I feel a sense of completeness and rightness I haven't felt in years.

It is the embrace of our souls.

Life is indeed a beautiful mystery, unpredictable and full of surprises.

As Julia and I sit close that night, everything feels right. It's like all the puzzle pieces of our lives have finally fit together.

When we tell Jim and Kim about us the next day, I'm a bit nervous. But Julia squeezes my hand, giving me courage.

"Kids," I say, "you know Jane, right? Jane's first name is Julia. We really like each other and will be together like a couple."

Kim's eyes light up. "Does this mean Julia will be here more?" she asks, hope in her voice.

"Yes, it does," Julia answers with a smile. "If that's okay with you."

Jim looks at us, then nods. "That's cool," he says, and I can tell he means it.

I look at Jim and Kim, their faces open and trusting, and take a deep breath. "Do you guys want Julia to be like your mom?" I ask gently.

Their smiles come quick and bright. "Yes," they both say, almost in unison.

Their simple, heartfelt response fills the room with a warmth that touches my heart. It's a moment full of love and hope, a sign that we're moving together into a new, happy chapter of our lives.

The room feels warm and happy. Later, watching Julia with the kids, I see how easily she fits into our family. It's like she was always meant to be here with us.

In bed, I recall little Julia's cute voice, "I will marry you when I grow up, Mr. Jones." I smile from the bottom of my heart before I fall asleep.

My Kiddie, Parrot, and Firefighter

My Kiddie, Parrot, and the Firefighter

I push open the door of Pet Mart, balancing my ten-month-old baby boy, Jamie, on my hip. He's my little bundle of joy, the sunshine in my otherwise routine life as a single mom and teacher. I'm here for cat food.

As we step in, Jamie's giggles blend with a wave of laughter echoing from the back of the store.

Curious, I maneuver through the aisles, a familiar voice rising above the rest. It's Eric, my next-door neighbor. He's a firefighter known around our small town for his bravery, pranks, and boundless humor.

There he stands, a crowd gathered around him, a parrot perched on his shoulder.

"Come on, Shakespeare, say 'hippopotomonstrosesquipedaliophobia,'" Eric coaxes, his eyes twinkling with mischief.

The word, meant to be funny because it's about fearing long words, confuses the parrot. It just squawks instead of repeating it, making everyone laugh again. I know parrots are clever, but the word Eric picked is too hard—even my middle school students would struggle to say it.

Jamie claps his hands, clearly entertained.

I can't help but smile. Eric's antics have a way of lighting up any room.

A red-haired young salesperson approaches me, assisting with placing a bag of cat food into my shopping cart. However, her somber expression casts a shadow over her helpful gesture.

"The poor parrot has been here too long. If no one buys it by today, we have to put it down," the salesperson says quietly, a frown on her face.

I look at the parrot, then at Jamie. I'm busy enough with my boy and a black cat, but I cannot watch the parrot die.

"I'll buy it," I say decisively.

The salesperson looks surprised, then relieved. "Really? Oh, thank you!"

The salesperson happily leads me to the parrot. "This bird is sold."

Eric overhears and turns to me, a broad grin on his face. "Look at you, Lucy, always the hero. First teaching our future generations, now saving parrots from my torture."

I roll my eyes, though I'm fighting back a smile. "Someone's got to counteract the trouble you cause."

Eric's chuckle ripples through the air, and he steps closer, his playful manner easing into a gentler tone. "Let me help you with the adoption. It's the least I can do for our new feathered friend."

Eric fills the air with jokes and easygoing chatter as we approach the counter. He's a natural entertainer—not just with Jamie, whose giggles echo in response to Eric's funny faces, but also with everyone around us. The customers nearby can't help but smile at his antics, and even the cashier looks amused, a break from her day's routine. Eric's presence is like a beam of sunlight, warming everyone it touches.

"All right, Shakespeare, welcome to Team Lucy," Eric announces, handing me the paperwork with a flourish. The parrot squawks, almost as if it understands and approves, sending another wave of laughter through the store.

"Thanks for the help, Eric," I say with genuine gratitude.

"Anytime, Lucy. And remember, if Shakespeare here gets cheeky, I'm just a shout away for a parrot pep talk," he replies with a wink.

I can't help but smile, shaking my head in amusement. "We'll be fine but thank you."

As we leave Pet Mart, the moment's warmth stays with us. Eric's grin never fades, and I am happy with my new pet. It's a simple yet comforting end to an unexpected adventure.

After the day at the pet store, I often run into Eric. Fate enjoys playing matchmaker with neighbors. His house, a kaleidoscope of colors and quirky garden gnomes, stands out next to my more subdued abode. Seeing him has become as regular as the morning paper.

On Saturday morning, while I'm lost in petunias and pansies, Jamie is in his baby car, happily gnawing on a teething toy. Eric jogs past, his smile bright enough to compete with the morning sun.

"Morning, Lucy! Is Shakespeare causing a ruckus yet?" he calls out.

I laugh, shaking my head. "That bird's a bigger drama queen than any of my middle school students!"

He pauses, resting his hands on the fence, his grin unwavering. "Need a hand? I've become quite an expert in bird psychology... and kiddie entertainment."

"No, thanks. We're somehow surviving the Shakespearean drama," I reply, touched by his offer, even if it's just neighborly politeness.

At that moment, Captain, my supposedly intelligent cat, decides to enact his great escape. He nudges the front door open with the finesse of a cat burglar and darts off, clearly mistaking himself for a feline James Bond. His target: the unsuspecting goldfish in Eric's pond. He zigzags along the fence line, then, with Olympic-level agility, leaps over into Eric's yard.

"Eric, quick! Captain's playing secret agent in your backyard!" I yell, a mix of amusement and alarm in my voice.

Eric springs into action, his jog turning into a sprint. Balancing Jamie on my hip, I follow him, curious and slightly anxious.

In Eric's backyard, we're greeted by the sight of Captain, now a proud conqueror, scaling an ancient oak tree. He ascends with the grace of a seasoned climber, reaching dizzying heights until he's just a rebellious dot against the sky.

I assume Captain will come down when bored, but a sudden, pitiful meow suggests otherwise. My heart sinks. He's stuck.

Eric glances at me, the corners of his eyes crinkling with amusement. "Captain wants to test the local firefighter's cat-rescuing skills."

He sheds his jacket, revealing a T-shirt titled "Local Hero at Work." In a few smooth motions, he's up the tree, moving confidently, making it look like a walk in the park. Reaching Captain, he gently coaxes my adventurous cat into his arms and begins the descent. He's back on solid ground in no time, looking every bit the hero from a Saturday morning cartoon.

"Your cat's quite the escapologist," Eric comments, setting Captain down. Now realizing his adventure wasn't as thrilling as anticipated, the cat scurries towards home, dignity slightly ruffled.

Eric's laughter is light and infectious. "Well, the fish had a narrow escape. I think they'll enjoy a vacation indoors for a bit."

"Thank you, Eric. I owe you big time," I say, relief washing over me.

His eyes twinkle with a familiar mischief. "Owe me? I'm a simple man. I accept payments in coffee. How about tomorrow?"

I hesitate, and then a smile breaks across my face. "Coffee it is." After all, how could I say no to my cat's dashing rescuer?

I have to call my babysitter to take care of Jamie tomorrow.

Having coffee with Eric is like accidentally walking onto a sitcom set filled with laughter. We're nestled in a corner of the local coffee shop.

Eric leans back, his chair creaking slightly under his weight. He continues his story loudly.

"So, there I was, right? Knee-deep in floodwater and this tiny pug is just yapping away on the roof of a car," he begins, his hands animating each word.

Initially engrossed in their own worlds, the surrounding patrons start glancing over, drawn by the magnetic pull of his storytelling. Laughter bubbles from his lips, infectious and hearty, and soon, it's not just our table but the whole room echoing with mirth.

"But you should've seen the owner's face, Lucy! Like I'd handed her a bar of gold instead of a sopping wet, disgruntled pug." He chuckles, eyes twinkling with the joy of sharing.

I offer a small, somewhat restrained smile, sipping my coffee. While Eric's tales are hilarious, the increasing attention from others makes me shrink inward. The spotlight, even by association, feels glaring on my introverted soul.

I enjoy Eric's company—his easy charm, his vivid recounting of everyday heroics. But I feel a mismatch. I crave stability, a specific educational parity, and a secure life.

"Hey, you've gone quiet on me," Eric observes, his smile softening into a look of concern. "Everything okay?"

I nod, forcing my smile to widen with just a touch. "Yeah, just... overwhelmed by the crowd, I guess."

He leans in, lowering his voice. "I sometimes forget how loud I can get. Sorry about that, Lucy. I don't mean to make you uncomfortable."

"It's not just that," I murmur, fidgeting with the handle of my cup.

Eric's expression shifts to one of understanding, tinged with a hint of disappointment. "I get it," he says, nodding slowly. "You need someone who's more your speed. Guess I'm a bit too much of a free spirit, huh?"

A bittersweet smile crosses my lips. "Maybe just a bit."

The following weekend, my kitchen turns into a scene straight out of a sitcom. Water cascades from the dishwasher, turning my cozy nook of yellow walls and potted plants into a miniature lake. The wooden cabinet under the sink, soaked through, looks like it's decided to take an impromptu swim.

I'm frantically throwing towels onto the ever-expanding puddles when a knock at the door startles me. Swinging it open, I find Eric, an armful of misdelivered mail in his grasp.

"Looks like the mailman's playing puzzles with house numbers again," he says with a grin, which quickly falls away as he steps into the aquatic chaos of my kitchen. "Whoa, do you need a plumber or an ark?"

His light tone is a stark contrast to the flood's severity. "At this point, I'd take either," I reply, my voice laced with stress.

Eric doesn't miss a beat. He dives under the sink to turn off the water valve, then darts out and returns, toolbox in tow, wading into the water with an almost comical determination.

While he battles the rebellious plumbing, I retreat to check on Jamie, who's blissfully ignorant of the chaos. Eric's muffled instructions to Shakespeare, my unusually quiet parrot, drift from the kitchen.

Curiosity piqued, I tiptoe back, only to discover Eric, now ankle-deep in water, animatedly chatting with Shakespeare. "Repeat after me, 'Eric is the best plumber,'" he instructs, a mischievous sparkle in his eye.

I can't help but laugh, the absurdity of the situation is cutting through my stress. "Really, Eric? A parrot plumber's apprentice?"

He shoots me a grin, his hands still busy with the pipes. "Hey, everyone needs a sidekick. Shakespeare's got potential."

The crisis eventually subsides, and my kitchen returns to its usual dry state. In relief and gratitude, I hand Eric a box of candy. "For your heroic plumbing skills... and the unique entertainment."

He winks, accepting the treat. "Anytime. I'm all about saving the day—or causing harmless chaos."

It's only the next day, returning from work, that I'm greeted by Shakespeare's new phrase: "Eric is the best match." The bird's imitation of Eric's voice is uncanny.

Shaking my head, I scribble a note to Eric and leave it at his door, a playful jab at his latest antic: "Parrot brainwashing is not neighborly."

Despite everything, how Eric seamlessly blends into my life is starting to make an impression on me. His humor and readiness to help, without a moment's hesitation, are hard to ignore.

Our coffee date fades into memory, and life resumes its comfortable rhythm, with Eric weaving himself into the fabric of my days. His jokes and easygoing nature become a familiar presence. Yet, I find myself at a crossroads when he suggests moving beyond casual meetups.

I'm cautious, torn between the warmth of gratitude and the pulse of something more profound. In my quieter moments, I envision a future husband who is not just kind but also brings the stability of education and a steady career. With his laughter and lightness, Eric offers solace but not the security I crave.

One bright afternoon, while I'm absorbed in the dance of gardening, Eric's voice drifts over the fence. "Hey, Lucy, how about dinner tonight?"

The question catches me mid-prune. I look up, meeting his hopeful eyes. "Eric, you're wonderful, but I don't see us like that. I'm sorry."

His smile doesn't falter, but there's a fleeting shadow in his eyes that he quickly masks. "No worries, Lucy. Worth a shot, right?"

This scene becomes a recurring motif: Eric, undaunted, finds creative ways to ask me out—a bouquet of flowers one day, a handcrafted invitation another. Each refusal I offer is tinged with a blend of affection and guilt.

In the meantime, my thoughts increasingly linger on Daniel, a CPA I met at a recent teacher's conference. His lecture on tax strategies was insightful and delivered with a charming blend of intelligence and wit. He seemed to embody the qualities I yearned for—knowledgeable, kind, and grounded.

Yet, dating as a single mom is a puzzle, with pieces like childcare always needing to be placed, and sometimes the babysitter is unavailable at short notice.

One evening, while contemplating this, an idea forms. A gesture of gratitude towards Eric: a homemade cake for his continuous understanding and support.

Holding the cake, I knock on Eric's door. He greets me, his face lighting up at the sight of the dessert... and perhaps a little at seeing me.

"Is this a peace offering?" he teases, accepting the cake.

"In a way," I laugh. "Actually, I have a favor to ask."

His eyebrows arch in interest. "Oh? What is it?"

"I have a date this weekend. Could you… maybe babysit Jamie?"

The surprise in Eric's eyes is evident but swiftly replaced by a warm smile. "Of course, I'd love to. Jamie and I are going to have a great time."

The date with Daniel is a mix of nerves and excitement. Returning home, I find Jamie asleep, a contented smile on his face. Looking happy and tired, Eric shares stories of their evening's adventures. His enthusiasm and the warmth in his voice bring me unexpected joy.

"Thanks, Eric. I really appreciate this," I say, feeling deeply grateful.

"Anytime, Lucy. Jamie's a great kid, and you're an amazing mom," he responds, his sincerity resonating with me.

As I close the door behind me, a wave of gratitude and something else—a flicker of doubt—washes over me. Unbeknownst to me, this evening has set in motion a chain of events that will challenge my perceptions, mainly as Daniel's first visit draws near.

On Sunday afternoon, when I meet Daniel at the park, Daniel unexpectedly requests to visit my home. He wants to meet Jamie and see where we live, a sudden but understandable request from someone as methodical as him.

As Daniel and I walk into my living room, the familiar warmth of home greets us—soft couches, Jamie's scattered toys, and the walls adorned with family memories. Eric is also sitting cross-legged on the floor, deeply engaged in a block-building mission with Jamie.

"Hey, Lucy! And this must be Daniel," Eric says, his voice blending warmth and welcome.

Daniel politely nods, his gaze taking in the scene with a calculative air. "Nice to meet you. Your name?"

"Eric. My name is Eric."

Jamie, spotting Eric, abandons his blocks and toddles over with a bright smile. "Dad!" he exclaims, reaching up to him.

The word hangs in the air like a misplaced note, and I see Daniel's brows furrow in confusion. "Dad? Why is he calling Eric that?"

I rush to clarify, feeling the tension rise. "Oh, Eric's just a good friend from next door. Jamie adores him."

Daniel's eyes don't stray from Eric, his voice laced with professional skepticism. "Is that so?"

Before I can further smooth the ruffled feathers, Shakespeare, ever the opportunist, chimes in from his perch. "Eric is a good match!" he squawks, repeating his newfound favorite phrase.

I laugh nervously, trying to lighten the mood. "This parrot, I swear, becomes a chatterbox whenever we have visitors."

But the damage is done. Daniel's expression shifts from mild curiosity to something more intricate, more calculating. "A neighbor and a parrot are both quite... involved in your family life, it seems."

Struggling to keep my tone light, I respond, "It's really not what it looks like, Daniel."

Eric rises to his feet, his face etched with concern. "Honestly, Daniel, it's just fun with Jamie and the bird. Nothing serious."

Daniel's eyes linger on Eric, then shift to me, his voice laced with a hint of disapproval. "Lucy, our relationship should be built on transparency. This is... unexpected."

Stammering, I attempt to dispel his doubts. "Daniel, please, you're misunderstanding the situation."

Daniel's posture stiffens, his expression morphing from curiosity to suspicion. "I see. "

My attempts to smooth things over are desperate. "Daniel, it's not what it seems. Eric has been a great help, but that's all there is to it."

Eric stands, dusting off his hands. "She's right, Daniel. I just enjoy hanging out with Jamie. No hidden agendas."

Daniel's response is measured, his CPA-like precision surfacing. "A neighbor teaching your child to call him Dad, and a parrot echoing sentiments of compatibility. You must admit, it's peculiar."

I feel my face flush with frustration. "It's just a misunderstanding, nothing more."

Daniel regards me with a look that weighs and measures my words. "I value honesty, Lucy. This feels less than straightforward."

Sensing the gravity of the situation, Eric takes a step towards Daniel. His usual playfulness is replaced by a seriousness rarely seen. "Look, Daniel, I didn't mean to cause any confusion. I care about them, sure, but just as friends and neighbors."

Daniel's gaze shifts between Eric and me, weighing his words.

I'm stammering now, trying to find the right words. "Daniel, please understand it's not what you're thinking."

Daniel looks at me, his expression one of calculated decision. "I appreciate honesty above all, Lucy. This situation seems muddled."

With a curt nod, he makes his way to the door, his steps deliberate. "I thought we had a transparent understanding. I may have been mistaken."

His departure leaves a void filled only by the echo of the closing door. Shocked, I sink into the nearest chair, my mind racing.

Eric kneels beside me, his voice soft. "Lucy, I'm so sorry. I didn't mean for any of this to happen."

I look up at him, his genuine concern contrasting Daniel's calculated withdrawal. "It's not your fault, Eric. It's just... complicated."

As Eric nods understandingly, I can't help but wonder about the striking differences between the two men. One is so quick to bring joy and ease into our lives, and the other is so quick to judge and depart at the first sign of complexity.

Eric, also surprised, sits down next to me, his characteristic cheerfulness subdued by the gravity of the situation.

"Lucy, I was just trying to add a bit of humor to Jamie's day. I never imagined it would lead to this," Eric says, his voice laden with sincere regret.

In the aftermath of Daniel's departure, I find myself deep in thought, Eric's presence a comforting constant beside me.

The contrast between Eric's playful, caring nature and Daniel's rigid, unforgiving demeanor becomes strikingly clear.

"Lucy, I know I can be a bit much sometimes," Eric begins, his voice soft and earnest. "But I care about you and Jamie, genuinely. I just want to bring a little happiness to your lives."

I look at him, seeing the truth in his eyes. "Eric, you've always been there, making us laugh, helping out. You've been more of a partner than I realized."

He nods a gentle kindness in his gaze. "Life's too short not to spread a little joy, Lucy. Especially to those who deserve it most."

As the evening unfolds, Eric helps put Jamie to bed, his gentle way with my son further warming my heart. We then sit down to share dinner. Our conversation flows more deeply than ever before.

As the night draws closer, Eric moves towards the doorway, signaling it's time for him to head home. He pauses and turns to me, his expression warm and filled with sincere reassurance. "Actually, I've grown really fond of Jamie. I truly hope, one day, he might come to call me 'Dad.'"

Watching him leave, a sense of clarity washes over me. With its unexpected events, this chaotic evening has shed light on what truly matters in a relationship.

The support, the care, the laughter Eric brings into our lives. A man's kind nature is more valuable than book-smart in real life.

What I've been looking for has been here, with Eric, all along.

The following weekend, after my heart-to-heart with Eric, my phone buzzed with an unexpected call. It's Daniel. My heart skips a beat, a mix of surprise and unease settling in. I take a deep breath and answer, bracing myself for the conversation.

"Lucy, I've been thinking," Daniel says, voice-controlled as always. "I believe we might have acted hastily. I'd like to meet and discuss things."

His words hang in the air, a proposition I wasn't prepared for. But at this moment, with new-found clarity and the warmth of my feelings for Eric still fresh, my decision is evident.

"Daniel, I appreciate your call, but I don't think there's anything left to discuss," I reply, my voice firm yet polite.

There's a pause, and I can almost picture Daniel's brows knitting together in confusion. "Are you sure? I think we could work things out, reconsider—"

I cut him off gently but resolutely. "I'm sure, Daniel. My decision is final. I'm moving forward, and we both should do the same."

There's a brief silence, a sign that my words have registered. "Well, if that's your decision, then I wish you the best, Lucy," he says, his voice revealing a hint of disappointment.

"Thank you, Daniel. I wish you the best too."

As I end the call, I feel relief. Standing by my decision and choosing my own path feels empowering. I glance over at Jamie, playing with his toys. I've made the right choice for us all. Eric will be a good father.

Later that day, I stand outside Eric's door with Jamie, my palms sweaty and my heart racing. This is it, the moment of truth. I knock, and he answers, his face lighting up as he sees me.

"Lucy, everything okay?" he asks, concern flickering in his eyes.

I take a deep breath, finding the courage to speak my truth. "Eric, I need to tell you something. It's important."

He steps aside, inviting me in. We sit on his couch, the room bathed in the warm afternoon light, creating an intimate atmosphere.

"I've ended things with Daniel," I begin, my voice trembling slightly. "And it's made me realize something important. I... I have feelings for you, Eric. But I'm scared. Scared of rushing into something, of getting it wrong."

Eric reaches out, his hand covering mine, a tender gesture sending shivers down my spine. "Lucy, I've cared about you for a long time. But

I'll go at whatever pace you're comfortable with. There's no rush. I just want to be with you, to make you and Jamie happy."

His words, so simple but sincere and full of warmth, make my heart swell. The uncertainty holding me back melts away, replaced by a growing hope and excitement.

"Eric, you've brought so much joy and laughter into our lives. I want to see where this goes with you," my voice soft but filled with emotion.

He smiles. It's a smile that reaches his eyes, radiating pure joy.

"Lucy, that's all I've ever wanted. "

Eric walks me back to my house, gently cradling Jamie in his arms. His manner is tender and protective, like a father carrying his child.

In the soft glow of the evening, Eric and I sit together on my backyard porch, the air filled with the sweet scent of blooming jasmine. The setting sun paints the sky in shades of orange and pink, creating a romantic backdrop to our quiet conversation.

"Lucy, I know we've both been through a lot," Eric starts, his hand finding mine, his touch sending a warm thrill through me. "But I want to do this right, take it slow, make sure it's built on a strong foundation."

I nod, my heart swelling with emotion. "I want that too, Eric. To build something real and lasting together."

We sit there, hand in hand, watching the stars begin to twinkle in the evening sky. The warmth between us is palpable, a promise of things to come.

I lean closer to Eric and feel he is my rock. Our lips meet in a tender kiss, a perfect seal to our shared hopes and dreams.

The security offered by a man's golden heart, warm and invaluable, far surpasses the cold comfort of mere book smarts.

Harmonies and Heartbeats

I'm engrossed in practicing my singing, hitting some challenging high notes, when I suddenly hear an off pitch wailing outside. It sounds like... is that a dog trying to mimic my singing?

Annoyed, I stomp to the window, preparing to give the owner a piece of my mind. But as I pull it open, the sight before me causes my annoyance to give way to giggles. My new neighbor, a handsome guy, is lounging on his patio swing chair, and next to him is a massive dog, head thrown back, belting out his version of my song.

"Um, excuse me?" I call out, trying to stifle my laughter. "Your dog seems to think he's the next big thing in opera?"

The neighbor looks up, startled, and then breaks into a sheepish grin. "Oh! I'm so sorry. That's Thunder. He gets a little carried away when he hears music. Thinks he's a canine Pavarotti or something."

"I can see that," I reply with a smirk. "I mean, I've had fans before, but this is a first."

He chuckles, "Well, it looks like you've got yourself a new duet partner. By the way, I'm Rober. The charming new addition to this community."

Laughing, I reply, "Lana. The already charming resident. Welcome to the madhouse!"

"Pleasure to meet you, Lana. And apologies again for Thunder's... um... performance."

"Tell Thunder he might need a few more lessons before his big debut," I tease.

Rober chuckles, patting Thunder's head. "Hear that, buddy? You've got work to do."

We share a friendly wave, and I return to practice, silently hoping for more interruptions from my amusing new neighbors.

Before I close my window, Whiskers, my Russian Blue cat, jumps to the windowsill and touches me with his head. His green eyes tell me it's time for him to play outside.

Sunlight filters through the curtains as I start my vocal warm-ups. The notes flow smoothly, and the rhythm is right on point. My primary performance is just around the corner, and every practice counts. As I hit a high note, I'm rudely interrupted by a series of deep, booming barks.

Not again.

Thunder. That big, adorable, incredibly noisy furball. Why did he pick my singing time to showcase his vocal range? I try to continue, hoping he'll stop, but the barks grow louder and more insistent, matching my pitch and rhythm.

Enough is enough. Marching to the window, I fling it open, ready to confront the canine opera singer. But instead, I lock eyes with Rober, lounging on his patio swing chair, seemingly enjoying the ruckus.

"Really?" I start, my tone sharp, trying to hide my obvious annoyance. "Is this a daily duet now?"

Rober smirks, looking unfazed. "Ah, Lana! Thunder here seems to think you guys could form the next hit duo. You know, bring a bit of canine charm to the music world."

"This is hardly the time for jokes, Rober," I retort, hands on my hips. "I have an important performance in a few days. I can't afford these... disruptions."

He raises an eyebrow, a playful glint in his eyes. "Ah, c'mon, it's just a bit of fun. Besides, it's good to have a backup singer, right?"

"I need silence, not a barking 'backup'!" I exclaim, my patience thinning. "You need to control your dog. And for the record, a good owner would teach his dog manners."

Rober's smirk fades, replaced with a touch of defiance. "Hey now, Thunder's just being himself. Can't fault him for having a bit of musical flair. Maybe you should try embracing it."

I'm flabbergasted. "Are you serious right now? Your dog is disturbing the peace, and you're defending him?"

He chuckles. "Well, when you put it that way…. But Lana, he's still getting used to the place. Give him some time."

I take a deep breath, reminding myself to stay calm. "Rober, I'm all for animals being themselves. But not at the cost of my practice. Not when it jeopardizes my performance."

He leans back, looking thoughtful. "All right, point taken. But you've got to admit, his barks have a rhythm."

I sigh, trying hard not to smile. "You're impossible, you know that?"

He grins. "Been told that before. We'll work on the barking. No promises on the singing, though."

We share a brief moment of understanding before I close the window, hoping for a more peaceful practice session next time.

The evening sun casts a golden hue, enveloping the neighborhood in a serene warmth. I enjoy a quiet moment on my patio when an unexpected commotion shatters the peace. It's Whiskers' alarmed meow, unmistakable and urgent. I spring up, my heart pounding, to find my beloved cat being chased by Thunder, who looks like he's having the time of his life.

To escape the massive dog, Whiskers climbs up a tree, her eyes wide with fear, her tail bushy, and her body pressed close to the branch. I can hear her terrified meows echoing in the stillness of the evening. Thunder sits below, wagging his tail, seemingly pleased with the chaos he's caused.

Adrenaline courses through my veins, and I'm livid. Without a second thought, I storm towards Rober's house, not caring that I'm still in my pajamas, and bang on his door.

A few moments later, Rober, looking bewildered, opens up. Before he can utter a greeting, I point accusingly toward the tree. "Your dog has scared Whiskers half to death!"

Rober looks in the direction I'm pointing, taking in the scene. He seems to stifle a laugh but quickly turns it into a cough. "Ah, it seems Thunder is making friends," he quips, his tone light, but I'm not in the mood for humor.

"Making friends? Your dog is terrorizing my cat! Whiskers is terrified!"

Rober raises an eyebrow, then sighs, his humorous facade dropping. "I'm sorry, Lana. I genuinely am. Thunder has a playful spirit; he didn't mean any harm."

"Playful spirit? My cat is up a tree, terrified because of your dog! You need to control him."

Rober looks apologetic. "I'll get Thunder inside and help get Whiskers down. I promise I'll work on keeping him in check."

We head outside together. Rober calls Thunder, who obediently follows him inside. Once sure that the threat is gone, I coax Whiskers down. Her petite frame trembles in my arms, her heart racing.

Rober stands beside me, a sheepish look on his face. "I'm really sorry, Lana. This won't happen again."

I give him a sharp look, but my anger is slowly dissipating. "It better not. Whiskers doesn't need this kind of excitement in her life."

He chuckles, "Neither does Thunder, it seems. Let's call it a truce?"

I sigh, nodding, "Truce. But keep Thunder away from Whiskers."

He salutes. "Will do, ma'am."

"Rober, do you know how to train your dog? There's a training school only a few miles away—"

"I don't think it is necessary," Rober interrupts me and rejects my suggestion directly.

I look at his handsome face and impressive muscular body, wondering what kind of father he could be if he had a kid.

"Imagine something about me?" Rober senses my thought.

"Yes. I want to know how badly you will spoil your kid if you luckily have one."

"Wow." He laughs. "Do you want to know how badly I will spoil the beautiful girl who will help me to produce the kid?"

His electric-blue eyes are shining and charming. I unexpectedly feel my heart skip a beat. I turn around and carry my cat home.

I have never had this feeling before. From that moment, I start avoiding Rober. I also try to lock my cat inside of my home.

The weekend arrives. It is my performance day.

The park is alive with the festive atmosphere of the art show. Vibrant colors, delicious smells, and the distant strumming of a guitar fill the air. As I step onto the stage, adjusting my microphone and scanning the crowd, my gaze locks on to a familiar pair—Rober and Thunder. They're seated in the front, looking quite the comedic duo: Rober with a dashing hat and Thunder sporting a little bowtie, making them stand out amid the spectators.

Taking a deep breath, I mentally prepare for my performance, but there's a nagging thought. What if Thunder decides this is the perfect backdrop for his singing debut? My nervous energy, however, seems misplaced as I begin. Thunder sits still, his big brown eyes locked on to mine, with an expression that says, "Don't worry, I've got your back."

As the melodies flow, I get lost in the music, my voice harmonizing with the instruments. The performance feels magical. As the last note lingers in the air and the crowd erupts in applause, I can't help but smile, relieved that Thunder maintained his gentlemanly demeanor throughout.

Walking off stage, I'm greeted by Rober, his face beaming. "That was amazing, Lana!"

I grin. "Thanks for keeping Thunder... quiet."

Rober chuckles. "I told him it was a 'listening' concert. He's a good listener, especially when treats are involved." Hearing his name, Thunder offers a playful wave of his tail, looking up at me as if seeking approval.

I bend to pat him. "Thanks for behaving, big guy." Thunder responds by licking my hand, which makes me laugh.

Seizing the moment, Rober says, "You must be starving after that stellar performance. How about lunch? There's this fantastic food truck I've been wanting to try."

"I'd love to," I reply, my stomach growling in agreement.

A tantalizing aroma of grilled sandwiches fills the air as we walk towards the food truck. We each get a sandwich, and Rober, the gentleman, finds us a shaded spot under a tree. Thunder sprawls out beside us, clearly enjoying the moment as much as we are.

Taking a bite of my sandwich, I mumble, "This is delicious."

Rober grins. "Told you. Nothing but the best for the star of the day."

We chat and laugh, and there's a lightness between us that wasn't there before. Maybe it's the music, or perhaps it's Thunder's newfound respect for my singing, but things feel different.

Rober, gazing intently, says, "I meant it, you know. You were incredible today. There's something about your voice—it's captivating."

I blush. "Thank you, Rober. That means a lot coming from you."

We share a moment, a mix of lingering eye contact and unsaid words, a delicate dance of emotions unfolding between us. Sensing the change in the atmosphere, Thunder lets out a tiny, comedic "woof," breaking our trance.

We both burst into laughter, the tension dissipating. Rober raises his sandwich. "To new beginnings?"

I tap my sandwich against his, adding, "And to Thunder, the most behaved dog at a concert."

The festival, filled with art and melodies, also hosts the budding rhythm of two hearts, tentatively finding their harmony.

After the festival performance, my life returns to my regular routine, but I have different feelings.

Every morning, predictably, Thunder is at my window. Each time I practice, this robust dog tries to harmonize with me. But it becomes something I anticipate with warmth. Our impromptu duets, once an interruption, now feel comforting. As I warm up to Thunder, my feelings for Rober also deepen.

One evening, as I return from a tiring rehearsal, Rober is standing outside his door. He quickly puts a finger to his lips, signaling me to be quiet, and points towards the bushes near my backyard.

I tiptoe closer, and my heart just melts. There they are, Thunder and Whiskers, supposed adversaries, curled up together in peaceful slumber. It's a scene straight out of a fairy tale.

Turning to Rober, eyes wide with delight, he whispers, "Looks like they're setting an example for us."

This newfound secret of our pets' unexpected bond brings us even closer. Evening coffees on the patio become our thing. I sit on his swing chair, discussing anything and everything. However, Rober remains a mystery in many ways. Any talk about his past, and he retreats. He's a firefighter—that much he shares. But there are shadows he's not ready to illuminate.

Sitting together one evening, I finally venture, "Rober, why do you never talk about your past?"

He hesitates, then says, "Some stories, Lana, they're better left untold. At least for now."

I nod, respecting his privacy. Before returning home, I look at his eyes, "Whenever you're ready to share, I'm here."

He gazes at me, eyes brimming with gratitude. "Thank you, Lana." Under the starlit sky, Rober looks into my eyes, stands up, walks to me slowly, and hugs me tightly.

It is our first hug. There's warmth, there's understanding, and two hearts are drawing closer.

I return home, the warmth of Rober's embrace still lingering. I'm lost in thought, replaying the comforting feel of his hug, when the jarring ringtone of my phone interrupts my daydream. Hesitantly, I pick up.

"Miss me?" The tone is smug, unmistakably Alex's. A shiver runs down my spine.

"Alex?"

"I've got a contract here, Lana. I can make you a star." He oozes confidence, but I sense the menace beneath his words.

"It's over. Stay away from me."

He chuckles darkly. "It's not over. You belong with me, Lana. With my guidance, you'll rise. Without it, you'll fade."

The pit in my stomach deepens. Alex needs to understand boundaries. "I don't need your 'guidance,' Alex. I've moved on. So should you."

The line goes dead.

A rush of adrenaline propels me to action. I hurriedly go around the house, locking all exterior doors and windows. Memories of our toxic relationship flash, and I feel trapped again. I know he can turn up unannounced, and I shudder at the thought.

That night is a nightmare for me.

Every creak and rustle outside send my heart racing as I anticipate his next move. I find it hard to shut my eyes, haunted by the day's events. The weight of fear threatens to pull me under, and the cold emptiness of the night seems almost unbearable.

As I'm about to give in to the overpowering dread, I feel a gentle nudge on my bed. Looking down, I see Whiskers, his large, round eyes full of concern. He hops up beside me, purring softly. He nudges his head against my hand, urging me to pet him. I pull him close, his soft fur providing some comfort.

Like a rhythmic lullaby, his consistent purring begins to soothe my jagged nerves. Whiskers, sensing my distress, snuggles closer, curling up beside me. His warmth and the gentle rise and fall of his breathing become my anchor to the present.

As the night wears on, the bond between us, the unspoken understanding, only grows. Whiskers doesn't leave my side, reminding me that amid all the chaos, there's still purity and love. His presence, steady and comforting, helps me brave the night, and I find solace in his quiet company.

The following day, I still cannot get rid of the fearful feeling. I need to tell someone, and

Rober instantly comes to mind. He's been my pillar of late, understanding and supportive. He needs to know about this.

The day is booked with my work. In the evening, as I'm returning from grocery shopping, a forceful grip catches my wrist in the dim light of my garage. I freeze, recognizing Alex's brooding silhouette.

"Lana," he murmurs, his voice low and threatening. "Thought I could surprise you."

Terrified, I attempt to muster every ounce of courage. "Let go of me, Alex!"

He smirks, squeezing my wrist even tighter. "You can't avoid me forever. I'm here to remind you where you truly belong."

"You're mistaken. I don't belong to anyone, especially not you!" My voice shakes with anger.

Without warning, a rapid sequence of events unfolds. From the shadows, a guttural growl precedes the lightning speed of Thunder's advance. The usually gentle giant now resembles a trained Army dog, lunging at Alex with unparalleled ferocity.

Alex, caught off guard, barely manages to side-step the first attack. But Thunder is relentless, snapping his jaws and cornering him against the garage wall.

"Get this beast off me!" Alex yells, panicked, but his arrogance is still unmistakably present.

Almost on cue, Rober emerges, his demeanor cold and determined, clearly showcasing his trained military background. "On your knees," he commands, advancing with an almost deadly grace.

Alex attempts a quick retort, but the combined threat of Rober and Thunder renders him momentarily speechless. Seizing the moment, Rober lunges, skillfully taking down Alex and pinning him to the ground, with Thunder growling beside them, ready to strike.

"Call the police," Rober tells me.

Soon, sirens wail in the distance, growing closer.

Two officers arrive swiftly, handcuffing a struggling Alex.

"You'll pay for this!" he spits venomously, his eyes darting between me and Rober with raw hatred.

One of the officers, clearly familiar with Alex's notorious reputation, remarks, "Looks like we finally got something solid on you."

As they lead him away, the tension that has filled the garage dissipates. I turn to Rober, overwhelmed with gratitude. "I can't thank you enough," I say, my voice shaky.

With a slight smirk, Rober replies, "All in a day's work. And Thunder deserves some credit too."

Sensing the shift in the atmosphere, Thunder trots over, wagging his tail, looking as if he hasn't just taken on a dangerous man.

Rober extends his hand, pulling me into a comforting embrace. "Promise me you'll be careful," he murmurs.

"I will," I reply, "especially with you and Thunder around."

The bond between us is palpable, solidified by danger and mutual respect.

***

The atmosphere in the dining room is thick with an unspoken understanding. The warm golden glow from the chandelier softens the room's edges, making it feel intimate and cozy. The gentle clinking of cutlery against plates is the only sound interrupting the comfortable silence.

After a few moments, Rober takes a deep breath, signaling he's ready to share something significant. "Lana," he begins, his voice lower than usual, "there's something about my past I've never really spoken about."

I look up, intrigued. His usually playful eyes now hold a depth of pain and remembrance. "Before the firefighting... I was a military dog trainer," he admits. I can see the memories playing out in his eyes as he continues, "Alice, she was my partner, my companion. Together, we navigated the treacherous terrains of Afghanistan. My bond with her was unlike anything I've ever felt."

The room is silent except for the faint chirping of crickets outside.

"We faced many perils together, evading land-mines, ambushes, and hostile forces. Alice was more than just a dog. She was a soldier, my pro-tector." He chokes up a bit, and I see him fight-ing back tears. "One fateful day, an ambush... she saved me, lunging at an enemy, taking a fatal shot meant for me."

I can't help the gasp that escapes my lips.

Rober's voice cracks as he continues, "Alice was a hero. She died so I could live. And Thunder...." He takes a deep breath. "Thunder is her off-spring, her legacy. Every time I look at him, I see Alice's brave eyes, her unwavering loyalty. That's why I spoil him; it's my way of honoring Alice's memory."

Tears well up in my eyes as I process his heart-wrenching story. I move closer, laying a comforting hand on his. Without a word, I kneel beside Thunder, who has quietly observed us. I wrap my arms around the massive dog, feeling the warmth and heartbeat of this living connec-tion to Rober's past.

"I promise," I whisper to Thunder, my voice thick with emotion, "I'll treat you like my child too, with all the love and care you deserve."

Rober watches, his eyes shining with a mixture of pain, gratitude, and a love deepening with each shared moment.

***

A few months later, the sun casts a warm orange hue, painting the sky with strokes of pink and gold. The scent of blooming roses fills the air, and the gentle chirping of the birds serenades us, making this moment seem almost surreal.

Setting up the camera on a tripod, I ensure it perfectly captures the dreamy evening sky. Whiskers is being his mischievous self, and I laugh, trying to make him sit still for the photo. On the other hand, Thunder sits obediently next to Rober, a true testament to his disciplined lineage.

With a twinkle in his eye, Rober declares, "All right, everyone. Let's say 'forever' on three!"

As the camera captures our smiles, Robert turns to me, his eyes reflecting the golden light. He's holding a small velvet box. My heart skips a beat.

"Lana," he says, trembling slightly with emotion, "you remember when we first met, right? Thunder howling, Whiskers causing chaos? Since then, every day with you has been something special. Whatever I've been through before doesn't compare to the thought of not having you by my side."

He opens the box, revealing a stunning diamond ring that catches the last rays of the setting sun. "Every day with you feels like a song, a melody I never want to end. Lana, will you marry me and make our song last forever?"

Tears blur my vision, every emotion bubbling up. "Yes," I reply, voice choked with emotion, "a thousand times, yes."

Sensing the gravity of the moment, Whiskers rubs against our legs with a contented purr. Thunder gives an affectionate bark. And as we lean in for a kiss, the camera's timer captures

this perfect moment—a promise of endless to-
morrows.

My Next Door Neighbor

Bang! Bang! The door shakes as Mr. Harlan, the landlord, pounds on it. His voice, rough like gravel, pierces through the thin walls of my small living room. "Lena! Open up! I know you're in there!"

I'm frozen, clutching the frayed hem of my apron. The room, cramped and cluttered with secondhand furniture, feels smaller with each knock. This is my world: stains on the carpet, a small TV blaring cartoons, and toys scattered around. I hear Tommy, my five-month-old boy, sniffling in the corner.

"Mommy, is the man mad?" Emily, my four-year-old, asks, her eyes wide and scared. I kneel, brushing her hair with my fingers, trying to smile.

"It's okay, sweetie. Go play with Tommy," I whisper, but my voice trembles.

Finally, I gather the courage to open the door.

Mr. Harlan stands there, his bulky frame blocking the sunlight. He's not a man who smiles since I signed the lease agreement. His face always set in a scowl, his green eyes sharp and unyielding.

"Lena, you're two months behind on rent. This can't go on," he barks, his voice echoing in the small hallway.

"I know, Mr. Harlan, I'm really trying to—" I start, but my voice is shaky, betraying my anxiety.

"Trying isn't paying, Lena. I've got bills too. I can't let you stay here for free." His tone is harsh, and I flinch.

But I do not hate him. He could have kicked me out last month if he only cared about his landlord's business. He must pay his home loan mortgage, property insurance, and taxes for his apartment.

Behind me, Tommy starts to wail, his cries mingling with the sound of a car honking outside. The noise of the big city, usually a background hum, feels overwhelming now.

"Please, I just need a little more time," I plead, my hands clasped together as if praying. "I've been looking for extra work, and I'm expecting some money soon."

Mr. Harlan sighs, his impatience evident. "I've heard that before. You've got until the end of the week, Lena. That's it. If you can't pay, I'll have to evict you."

My heart sinks. End of the week? That's just four days away.

I nod, unable to speak, fighting back tears.

Mr. Harlan turns and walks away, his steps heavy and final.

I close the door. Emily looks up at me, her small face filled with worry. "Are we going to have to leave, Mommy?"

I force a smile, though inside, I feel like crumbling. "No, baby, we're not going anywhere. Mommy will figure it out." I'm more likely to convince myself than her.

I look around the room at the sofa with a broken spring and the tiny water painting with a broken frame. All the valuable belongings were already traded for money. However, this is our home; no matter how shabby, it is our shelter. And the thought of losing it tightens my chest.

Tommy's cries grow louder. I scoop him up, bouncing him gently.

I need to be strong for them. I need to find a way. But as I rock my little boy, whispering soothing words, I can't help but wonder, how?

After Tommy falls asleep, I start housework. Dragging the trash bag, I step out into the chilly winter evening air. My mind is still reeling from Mr. Harlan's ultimatum.

Lost in thought, I almost bump into Andrew, my next-door neighbor. He's leaning against his doorframe, dressed in a faded leather that somehow adds to his "bad boy" charm.

He's handsome and doesn't try too hard, with a gentle edge to his rugged looks.

"Hey, Lena. Rough day?" His voice is smooth, with a hint of concern.

I force a smile, brushing a loose strand of hair behind my ear. "Just the usual," I keep it light, not wanting to dump my troubles on him.

He nods, his dark brown eyes thoughtful. "I overheard a bit. I'm sorry you're going through that."

There's a sincerity in his voice that takes me by surprise. In the big city, people usually care little about others' problems.

"Thanks, Andrew," I lift the trash bag, but it's heavier than I thought.

"Here, let me help with that." Before I can protest, Andrew takes the bag from me. His hands, rough and robust, like a prizefighter, do not match his software engineer job.

We walk to the dumpster, and the silence is smooth and comfortable in a strange way.

"If you ever need someone to watch the kids for a bit, I'm usually around," Andrew says casually as we walk back.

I'm taken aback. "Oh, I couldn't ask you to do that. You must be busy with work and all."

He chuckles, a sound that's warm and easy. "One of the perks of working from home. As an individual contractor, I've got a flexible schedule. And I don't mind, really."

I hesitate, torn. The offer is tempting, especially with my job hunt and the need for extra hours. "I'll think about it, Andrew. Thank you."

We reach our doors, and Andrew waves and smiles. "Anytime, Lena."

His offer echoes as I tuck Emily into bed that night. It's hard to trust someone with my kids, but there's something about Andrew that just feels right.

The following day, I find a note under my door: If you ever need me to babysit, just knock. -Andrew

It's the push I need. Later that day, I knock on his door, my heart racing. Andrew opens it, a warm smile on his face.

"Hey, Lena. Need that favor?"

I nod, feeling a mix of relief and nervousness. "Tomorrow morning, just for a couple of hours. I have a job interview."

"No problem." His encouragement feels genuine.

The following morning, I leave Emily and Tommy with Andrew, their giggles fading as I head down the hallway. As I walk to the interview, for the first time in a long while, I feel a glimmer of hope.

After the job interview, I rush home to pick up my kids. Then, I bake an apple pie to thank Andrew for his help. It's a small gesture, but it feels important to show my appreciation. The aroma of cinnamon and apples fills my cramped kitchen, offering a brief escape from my worries.

I carry the warm pie to Andrew's apartment, feeling nervous and excited.

Andrew opens the door with a surprised smile. "For me?" he asks playfully, his eyes lighting up.

"Yeah, just a little thank you for helping with Emily and Tommy," I reply, handing him the pie.

He invites me in, and I can't help but notice how his place contrasts with mine—tidy and modern with a personal charm.

"Thank you, but Tommy and Emily are waiting on some pie, too," I make an excuse. I'm so embarrassed to invite anyone to my own home. I'm a professional interior designer for goodness' sake.

I hurry back to my apartment, my heart racing with anticipation. The job interview went well, and I'm eager to check my email for updates. I switch on my computer, but it stubbornly refuses to boot up. I try again, frustration mounting. It's just another thing in a long list of things going wrong.

"Mom, is the computer broken?" Emily asks, peering over my shoulder with curious eyes. In the hard times, she is more mature than her age.

"I don't know, sweetie. Let me see if Andrew can help," I reply, trying to mask my worry.

I knock on Andrew's door, hoping he's home. He opens it with a smile that's both comforting and disarming. "Hey, Lena. Everything okay?"

"My computer's acting up. I'm waiting for an email about the job interview and...." I trail off, feeling a bit helpless.

"Let me take a look," he says, his tone light but reassuring.

In my apartment, Andrew examines the computer with a practiced eye. He clicks a few keys, his brow furrowed in concentration. "Looks like it just needs a little update and a reboot. I'll fix it."

As he works, I find myself watching him. There's a sense of calm about him, a quietly compelling confidence.

"You're really good at this," I remark.

He chuckles without looking up. "Well, it's part of my job. Can't let a computer beat me."

I laugh, the tension easing from my shoulders. "I used to be good at my job too, before... everything changed."

He looks up, his eyes gentle and understanding, encouraging me to keep talking. So, I do. I share my love for interior design and the business I built from scratch.

But I don't go into the part about how everything fell apart, about my husband leaving me for another woman. At the same time, I was pregnant with our son. It's a wound still too raw, and I'm not ready to expose that pain.

Andrew nods, listening intently. "Have you considered applying for assistance? It might ease the burden a bit."

I take a deep breath, feeling a mix of pride and vulnerability. "I've thought about it, sure. But I want to make it on my own first. I need to know that I can do this," I say, my voice steady despite the storm of emotions.

Andrew finishes with the computer and turns to face me, his expression one of genuine admiration. "You're courageous, Lena. Not everyone would keep pushing forward the way you do. It's impressive."

His words, so heartfelt, stir something profound inside me. I remember when sweetness and warmth were part of my everyday life, but those days are long gone. I'm no longer used to this kind of kindness, this acknowledgment of my struggles. It's a comforting and overwhelming feeling, a gentle reminder of a past I've had to leave behind.

"Thanks, Andrew. "I open the front door for him.

He smiles. "Anytime, Lena. And remember, if you ever need help or just someone to talk to, I'm next door."

Andrew leaves, and I realize how much his support means to me. Andrew sees my struggles and still believes in me. It is like a beacon in the darkness.

The morning light filters through the thin curtains, casting a soft glow on the piles of bills cluttering my kitchen table. Among them is a notice for a second job interview, but it's scheduled for ten days from now.

Today marks the end of the deadline Mr. Harlan, the landlord, gave me for the rent. It will be too late to save my situation even if I'm lucky enough to get the job.

Pay, or leave, by today.

A sharp knock on the door jolts me back to reality.

It's Mr. Harlan, the landlord, his expression grim. "Lena, I'm sorry, but I have no choice. I need to put an eviction notice on your door."

Panic rises in my throat as I face Mr. Harlan. "Please, just give me a bit more time. An eviction will ruin my credit," I plead with him.

"Lady, you don't have any credit to speak of," he retorts, his tone dismissive.

Just then, Andrew exits his apartment, interrupting the tense moment. "Mr. Harlan, how much does Lena owe?" His voice is steady, exuding a quiet confidence.

I'm stunned, watching as Andrew speaks with the landlord. Before I can muster a word of protest, Andrew has paid the overdue rent and the additional penalty. Mr. Harlan, looking somewhat perplexed, finally leaves.

I turn to Andrew, a mix of emotions swirling within me. "Andrew, why did you do that? I can't accept this." My voice is a blend of gratitude and embarrassment. The thought of owing Andrew, not knowing when or how I'll be able to repay him, fills me with a deep sense of shame.

"You needed help, Lena. It's okay to accept it sometimes," he replies reassuringly.

But I can't shake off the feeling of helplessness. I start looking for additional work, but it's almost impossible with two kids to care for.

Andrew notices my obvious distress. "Lena, a builder friend, wants someone to decorate a model home. I think you'd be a great fit for it."

This opportunity feels like a lifeline thrown to me in stormy seas. I eagerly accept the job, dedicating all my energy and creativity. My design receives glowing praise, leading to an official contract with the builder.

When my first paycheck arrives, I don't hesitate. I go straight to Andrew with a portion of the money. "I need to pay you back, at least partially, for now."

Andrew shakes his head, pushing my hand back. "Keep it, Lena. You earned it."

"No, Andrew. I can't keep owing you. Please," I say firmly.

After a moment, he accepts the money, understanding the importance of this gesture to me. "Okay, Lena. You win."

As he closes the door, I stand in the hallway, feeling relief and newfound confidence.

Working with that first builder marked a turning point in my life. Eventually, I secured contracts with several builders. It's a breakthrough that even allows me to afford a babysitter when I need to go out for work.

As the first rays of light brighten my life again, Tommy's first birthday arrives, bringing a sense of new beginnings and hope.

I'm hanging streamers in the small living room, the morning sun casting a soft glow on the faded wallpaper, when a knock at the door breaks my concentration. I open it to find Andrew, his arms laden with colorful balloons and a home-made cake.

"Happy birthday to Tommy," he declares, his smile reaching his eyes.

"Andrew, this... this is amazing," I stammer, overwhelmed by his thoughtfulness.

We work together, turning the living room into a little celebration haven. The balloons bob against the ceiling, and the cake, with its lop-sided icing, sits proudly on the table. Tommy's cute eyes widen in delight, and my heart fills with warmth.

As the kids play, Andrew and I find ourselves in the kitchen. He hands me a cup of coffee, our fingers brushing briefly. "You've done a great job with them, Lena," he says softly.

"Andrew, you were the one who opened the door for me. Now I'm working with multiple builders," I say, handing him the remaining money I owe him. A rush of gratitude fills me as I extend the envelope with a thank-you card to him.

This time, Andrew accepts the check without any argument, understanding the significance of this gesture.

We share a quiet moment inside the kitchen, the air between us charged with unspoken emotions. I find myself drawn to Andrew, our faces inches apart. My heart races, but fear grips me. I pull back, the memory of my past hurt flashing in my mind.

Andrew looks at me, understanding in his eyes. "It's okay, Lena," he says gently.

The rest of the day is a blur of laughter and birthday songs, but the moment in the kitchen lingers in my mind.

That night, lying in bed, I replay the almost-kiss. My heart aches with a mix of fear and longing. "I'm falling for him," I whisper into the darkness, the words both a confession and a realization.

I'm curious if he's awake, thinking about us. The thought makes my heart skip a beat.

The following day, I see Andrew in the hallway. "About yesterday...," I begin.

He smiles a little sadly. "No need to explain, Lena. I get it."

But I need him to know. "Andrew, I'm just… scared. I haven't felt this way in a long time."

He reaches out, taking my hand. "I'll be here, Lena. Whenever you're ready."

His touch is a promise, and I nod, my heart full of conflicting emotions—fear of being hurt yet hope for a new beginning.

As he walks away, I realize this is more than a fleeting attraction. It's deep, complicated, and genuine. But am I ready to take that leap again?

The newfound stability in my life feels like a warm embrace, a far cry from the chaos of the past. But just as I relax into this rhythm, life throws another curveball.

Andrew's been in a car accident!

My heart plummets as I hear this terrible news from a neighbor upstairs.

Dropping everything, I rush to the hospital, where I find Andrew with a broken leg and a

few bruises, but thankfully, nothing life-threat-
ening.

"Hey, Lena." He greets me with a weak but characteristic smile. "Looks like I won't be dancing
for a while."

His attempt at humor in the face of pain is like
him, and it warms and wrenches my heart. "You
better stick to software for now," I reply, trying
to keep the mood light.

When Andrew returns home, I help him with his
daily needs. It feels natural to care for him, and
a deep sense of connection grows between us.

Recalling Andrew's love for tranquil spaces, I
decide to use my interior design skills to trans-
form his bedroom into a more comfortable
place for his recovery. I select soft-colored wall
decorations, carefully crafting a serene sanctu-
ary where he can rest and heal.

When Andrew sees the transformation, his eyes
light up. "Lena, this is incredible. It feels like...
home."

His words strike me in a way I didn't antici-pate, unexpectedly revealing my hidden desire, a longing I hadn't fully acknowledged until now.

But with this realization comes a familiar fear. The thought of opening my heart again, espe-cially when life is just starting to stabilize, is daunting. The scars from my past relationship are still hidden beneath the surface.

One evening, as I'm leaving his apartment, An-drew reaches out and takes my hand. "Lena, I can't thank you enough. You've been my rock through all this."

I look into his eyes, seeing the sincerity and something more that speaks of shared mo-ments and unspoken feelings.

"I wanted to be here for you, Andrew," I say soft-ly, my heart aching with a mixture of emotions.

As I walk back to my apartment, my mind is a whirlwind of thoughts. The care I feel for An-drew is undeniable, but so is the fear of getting hurt again. It's a tug-of-war between wanting to leap into the possibilities of a new relationship and holding back to protect my fragile heart.

I must face these feelings, confront my fears, and decide what I want.

But as I close the door behind me, I realize that the crisis isn't just about Andrew's accident. It's about what awakened in me—a longing for love, companionship, and the courage to trust again.

As I help Andrew with his daily walk, a routine that has become a comforting part of our days, I feel closeness far beyond neighborly or friendly concern. His progress is slow but steady, a testament to his resilience.

Today, as we walk around the living room, Andrew's foot catches on the edge of the rug. He stumbles, and I instinctively reach out to catch him. Our bodies press close in the brief, panicked moment, and I can feel his heartbeat against mine.

"Whoa, that was close," Andrew breathes, steadying himself. His arm is still around my waist, and I'm acutely aware of how right it feels.

At that moment, all the emotions I've been holding back come rushing to the surface. "Andrew, I'm scared," I blurt out, the words tumbling from my lips before I can stop them.

He looks at me, concerned about me etching his features. "What's wrong, Lena?"

"It's just… I'm afraid of what's happening between us. I've been hurt before, and I don't know if I can go through that again," I confess, my voice trembling slightly.

Andrew's expression softens, and he gently takes my hand. "Lena, I understand. I've seen what you've been through and would never want to add to your pain."

His words are like a balm, soothing the raw edges of my fears. "I care about you, Andrew. More than I thought I would. But I'm just so afraid of getting hurt."

He nods, his eyes never leaving mine. "I care about you too, Lena. You and the kids. You've brought so much happiness into my life. I want to be there for you in whatever way you need."

The sincerity in his voice is unmistakable, piercing through the walls I've built around my heart.

"I want that too, but I need to take it slow. Can you understand that?" I ask, hoping he can sense the depth of my feelings despite my fear.

"Of course, Lena," he reassures me, and I feel a weight lift off my shoulders.

As we resume our walk, I feel a newfound sense of hope. The emotional revelation has brought us closer. For the first time, I'm not facing challenges alone.

Our understanding has blossomed into something beautiful, something that slowly and cautiously begins to look like dating.

Andrew and I start spending more time together, each moment filled with the tender exploration of a new and profoundly familiar relationship.

As Andrew's leg heals and my interior design business flourishes, I find myself overcoming the financial burdens that once seemed insurmountable. With each successful project, my credit rebuilds, and alongside it, my confidence grows.

One evening, Andrew suggests we go out to a nightclub. "It's time to see if this leg can handle a dance floor," he says with a twinkle in his eye.

The club is vibrant and alive, the pulsating music filling the air. As we step onto the dance floor, I feel excited. The lights flicker like stars, casting a magical glow over the dancers.

Andrew takes my hand, leading me into the rhythm of the music.

At first, we're both a bit awkward, mindful of his healing leg, but soon we find our flow. The music envelops us, and I find myself lost in the moment, in the feel of his hand in mine, his arm around my waist.

We dance close, the beat of the music matching the beat of our hearts. In the swirl of lights and sound, it feels like we're the only two people in the world. Andrew's smile is infectious, and I can't help but laugh, the sound mingling with the music.

As the song slows down, he pulls me closer, and we sway gently in each other's arms. I rest my head on his shoulder, feeling a sense of peace and contentment I hadn't thought possible. The music surrounds us, a soft cocoon in the bustling nightclub.

"This feels right, Lena," Andrew whispers, his breath warm against my ear.

"I never knew dancing could feel like this," I reply, barely above the music.

We stay like that for an eternity, wrapped in the melody and each other's embrace. The fears and doubts that once clouded my heart seem to melt away in his arms. I realize this is more than just a dance; it's a step towards a new life we're building together.

As we leave the nightclub, hand in hand, the cool night air feels refreshing against my skin. The city lights twinkle like distant stars, and I feel a deep sense of gratitude. For the first time in a long time, I'm not just surviving; I'm thriving in love and life.

***

A year has passed since Andrew and I started our journey together. Our love has grown, rooted in understanding and shared experiences, blossoming into something beautiful.

It's a crisp autumn evening, and Andrew has planned a picnic in the park. The leaves are a kaleidoscope of colors, painting a perfect backdrop. As we sit on a blanket, surrounded by the glow of lanterns he's hung from the trees, the world feels like it's ours alone.

"Lena, I have something I want to say," Andrew begins, his voice a mixture of nervousness and certainty.

He takes my hand, his eyes locking with mine. "This past year has been the best of my life. You've shown me what it means to love and be loved, to share life's burdens and joys. I can't imagine my life without you and the kids."

He reaches into his pocket and pulls out a small velvet box. My heart skips a beat as he opens it, revealing a simple yet elegant ring. "Lena, will you marry me?"

Tears well up in my eyes as joy overflows in my heart. "Yes, Andrew. Yes, I will marry you."

The proposal is simple, yet it's the most romantic moment of my life. Our embrace under the starlit sky seals our promise to each other.

Our wedding was small and intimate a few months later, just like we wanted. Close friends and family surround us as we exchange vows, the love and support palpable. Emily and Tommy stand by us, their faces alight with happiness.

As the celebration winds down, Andrew takes my hand, a mischievous glimmer in his eyes. "I have one more surprise for you," he says.

We drive through familiar streets until we pull up in front of a beautiful house, its windows glowing warmly in the evening light. My breath catches in my throat.

"I bought us a home, Lena. A place where we can make new memories without worrying about rent or instability. A place where we can grow old together," he says, his voice filled with emotion.

Tears stream down my face as I look at the house and then back at Andrew. This is more than just a house; it's a symbol of our new life, of the stability and love we've built together.

"Andrew, this is… I don't even have words. Thank you," I say, embracing him tightly.

As we stand there, in the embrace of each other, looking at our new home, I swear I will decorate our home with love.

Printed in Great Britain
by Amazon